HORRIBLE HARRY
Says Goodbye

Other Books by Suzy Kline

HORRIBLE HARRY
Says Goodbye

BY **SUZY KLINE**

PICTURES BY **AMY WUMMER**

VIKING

VIKING
Penguin Young Readers
An imprint of Penguin Random House LLC
375 Hudson Street
New York, New York 10014

First published in the United States of America by Viking, an imprint of
Penguin Random House LLC, 2018

Text copyright © 2018 by Suzy Kline
Illustrations copyright © 2018 by Penguin Random House LLC

LIBRARY OF CONGRESS CATALOGING-IN-PUBLICATION DATA IS AVAILABLE.
ISBN 9780451479631

Manufactured in China

1 3 5 7 9 10 8 6 4 2

DEDICATED WITH LOVE TO
my Horrible Harry readers

Contents

Snakes and Hairy Pennies

I remember when I first met Harry.

It was back in second grade.

He showed up with a snake in a box and made a girl scream.

I never liked those creepy crawly things he brought to school, but the earwig and spider weren't too bad. Harry always took good care of them.

For two years now, Harry's been my best friend.

We were supposed to be friends forever!

I knew we would be saying goodbye to third grade in a few days, and even to our favorite teacher. But I did *not* know about the *horrible* goodbye. That one is really too hard to write about, but I'll try.

It all started on a Friday in June, just when the South School dismissal bell rang.

"See you on Monday, kids!" Mrs. Flaubert said. "Our last day together in third grade!"

"Party!" Sidney blurted out. "Bring your Elvis music, Dexter!"

Dexter pretended to strum on a guitar while ZuZu pumped his arms in the air.

Song Lee and Ida started dancing. "Let's dress up like we're in the fifties!" Ida said. "We can wear skirts that twirl!"

"Yes!" Song Lee replied. "And I'm going to wear my party necklace."

When Dexter began singing "All Shook Up," one of his favorite Elvis songs, the girls started to rock and roll.

But not Mary. She was business as usual. It looked like she was making a beeline to our side of the room.

Harry and I were cleaning out our desks. When he pulled out a shrunken, burnt wiener, I cracked up. "Remember this, Dougo?" Harry asked.

I was laughing too much to answer.

Harry continued, "This baby was the

one that gave Sid the heebie-jeebies on our field trip at the copper mine!"

I nodded. "When we were way down in the dark cave . . . you tapped him on the shoulder with that wiener and freaked him out!"

"This thing is a fossil now!" Harry added with a toothy smile.

"It sure is," I replied, "but you know what, Harry? I wouldn't have been able to go down in that mine if it weren't for *you*."

"Really, Doug?"

"Yeah! Remember? You said to pretend I was a spider. They love dark cool places."

"And you went down in the dark!"

"I did!"

Harry and I tapped knuckles.

"Together!" I said. "And next year . . . in fourth grade, we're *both* going to be Safety Patrol Cadets!"

Suddenly, Mary appeared at our desks.

"Guys," she interrupted. "I have an important message. Mom and I are getting Mrs. Flaubert a gift certificate at Beyond Bath tomorrow for an end-of-the-year present. You two are the *only* people who have not made a contribution."

Harry and I looked at each other.

Oops! I thought.

I reached down in my right pocket and pulled out a five-dollar bill. "Sorry,"

I said. "I meant to give this to you yesterday."

"Thanks, Doug! You can sign the class card now." And she handed me a pen shaped like a flower. Song Lee had made the card. It said "World's Best Teacher" on the front and had a blue-and-gold felt ribbon—just like the kind you won at the state fair.

I printed my name and added a happy face with a Mohawk hairdo. I was planning to get that haircut during the summer.

"And *your* contribution?" Mary asked Harry.

Harry put both hands deep into his pockets and pulled out some pennies with hair and gum stuck to them, and one thin, green rubber snake.

Harry never had extra money. His parents were saving every dime for a new house. That's why they lived with his grandma. And why Harry never asked them for a penny or took home notices about things that cost money.

Mary rolled her eyes.

"Ewyee, gross!"

Harry shrugged. "So I'll bring my own bathroom gift on Monday for Miss Mack— Mrs. Flaubert!"

We could never get used to Miss Mackle's new married name!

Mary sighed. "I thought you'd probably say that. I bet you've got another crazy idea. Just *don't* bring toilet paper!" Then she took off.

Harry laughed as he pulled out what looked like a green saucer from his desk.

"This *was* green slime a month ago! It's all hard now. I guess it's coming with me—I can't leave anything behind!"

Then he popped that gross wiener fossil in his backpack, too.

Harry! I thought.

He could always make me smile.

We had only one day of school left—a party day—so what could possibly mess up the rest of my life?

The very next morning, I found out!

The Early Phone Call

*B*rrrring! Brrrring!

I opened one eyeball.

Who would be calling at this horrible hour?

Brrrring! Brrrring!

I looked at the Woody cowboy clock next to my bed. It said 6:30 a.m. On the fifth *brrrring*, I got out of bed and dragged myself into the kitchen.

"Hellooooo?" I said, picking up the phone.

"Dougo!"

It was Harry.

"How come you're calling so early?" I groaned. "It's Saturday! We can sleep in!"

"You have to see *what I see* outside my window. It's the biggest mystery ever!"

"Huh?" I said. "What big mystery?"

"Something is going on, Dougo, in that big old house next door to me. It's been

vacant for months, but now . . . *well,* you have to come over and see for yourself!"

"Now?" I moaned.

"Now!" Harry repeated. "Or you'll miss it!"

"Is your grandma even up?" I asked.

"Are you kidding? She's been up since four baking pies for people. Come on over!"

"I'll have to ask Mom."

When Harry gets an idea, there's no

stopping him. I was a bit curious about that empty house, though.

I went into my parents' bedroom. They were still sleeping, so I tapped Mom on the shoulder. When she turned her head toward me, her eyes were barely open. "Who was that on the phone?"

"Harry. He wants me to come over. Can I?"

"Grab a banana before you go," she replied. Then her head plopped back down on the pillow.

"Thanks, Mom," I said.

The Mystery House

As I hopped onto my bike and rode down my driveway, something caught my eye from across the street.

I dropped both feet to the pavement and forced myself to stop.

There it was sparkling in the morning sunlight. . . .

A brand-new "House for Sale" sign.

Whoa . . . I thought!

How cool would it be if Harry could

move into *that house*! We would be best friends *and* neighbors!

I jumped onto my bike pedals and sped off just thinking about it! I went racing down the street, past South School and around the corner to Harry's house.

When I got closer, I could see him sitting on his grandma's front steps waiting for me. There were a bunch of

cars parked at the empty house next door.

The Goog, Harry's cat, was sitting proudly on Harry's lap. He only had one eye, but he didn't seem to mind. The other one was sewed up after an accident. I parked my bike on the lawn and joined them on the stoop.

"What's going on?" I asked, petting his cat's gray-and-black-striped fur. The Goog started purring. There were two

station wagons on the front lawn and three SUVs in his neighbor's driveway.

"An army of people just came about an hour ago, carrying all kinds of boxes and stuff like mops and brooms into that old house," Harry explained. "Hear anything?"

I listened for a moment. The Goog seemed to have his own motor going.

"I just heard a *vroom vroom!*" Harry exclaimed. When he jumped up, the Goog made a flying leap into the air, landing on the lawn on all four paws. He arched his back, then scampered through the cat door into the house.

"I'm checking it out," Harry said, heading over to the mystery house.

I followed him. When he got there, he stood on his tiptoes and peeked in the side window. "Take a look, Dougo!" he ordered. "You can see much better over here."

"Harry!" I replied. "We can't spy on these people! They may be your new neighbors!"

"These people aren't the new neighbors," Harry said. "There's too many of them. Last count was thirteen!"

"They're probably cleaning up the place for the people who are coming," I explained. "That's not rocket science!"

"They're not professional movers," Harry answered. "Most of them look like my grandma. They all have white or silver hair! Except for the woman who just turned on the vacuum cleaner. She's six feet tall with black hair piled on her head."

I joined Harry at the window to get a better look. I stared in at the tall lady doing a jig as she sashayed across the living room floor with a vacuum cleaner. She looked familiar!

"*Harry Spooger!*" his grandma called. She was standing in her front doorway with something on a big plate. "You get back here right away!"

Harry and I quickly turned around and ran for his house.

"You know you don't go snooping on people!" she scolded.

After we nodded, she added, "So what did you see in that old house?"

Harry chuckled. His grandma was as curious as we were! "People cleaning up. Someone very special must be moving in soon. Do you have any idea who it is?"

"I'm hoping it won't be a rascal like you!" she joked, handing us her plate and two glasses of milk. "Eat these elephant ears while they're still warm."

Then she went back into the house.

"Elephant ears?" I said. "They sure smell good!" I started to drool over the melted butter and sugary glaze on top of a big slab of golden brown crust.

"I love 'em," Harry said as he took a big bite into one. "Grandma always makes them with her leftover pie dough. That's the best part of having a bakery in our kitchen—the leftovers! Got to be here early though. They go fast!"

My crispy piece melted in my mouth. I was glad Harry's grandma provided seconds and a tall glass of milk.

As Harry and I sat on that stoop enjoying our snack, a jeep drove up. A woman got out and walked over to the mystery house. She yanked the "House for Sale" sign out of the lawn and tossed it into the back of her car.

"Who's moving in?" Harry shouted.

The lady looked over and waved. "A big, wonderful family!"

"Any kids?" Harry called back.

"Seven!"

"Seven? Well, hot dog!" Harry exclaimed. "That's enough to make a baseball team!"

The lady smiled as she slammed the trunk. "You may have to teach them how to play the game though," she said.

Harry grabbed his second elephant ear. "Who doesn't know how to play baseball in America?" he asked me.

"I guess this *is* your biggest mystery!" I replied.

Harry's Room

"It *is* my biggest mystery!" Harry agreed. Then he lowered his voice. "Let's go inside, Dougo! We can spy out of my bedroom window and see what's happening in the backyard."

"Yes!" I replied, doing a trucker's beep with my right arm. I loved going to Harry's room. It was like the coolest museum! He was always adding something new.

As we hurried through the living room, I noticed the Goog. He was all curled up in a ball on their couch next to a pillow that said "Laugh and Love." He probably knew he wouldn't be interrupted there.

Harry's grandma was taking a pie out of the oven. It smelled like apples and brown sugar.

Harry had a hard time opening the door to his room. There were piles of clothes and stuffed animals on the other side. We had to squeeze our bodies around the door to get in.

An ant farm was sitting on the floor, but it just had sand. "I ordered ants from California," Harry said when he saw me looking at it. "They should come any day now, hopefully with the queen!"

Harry's small fish tank was on top of his dresser. It had two gross snails, but I liked the bubble head goldfish. Slink, his garter snake, was in his "hide box," which was 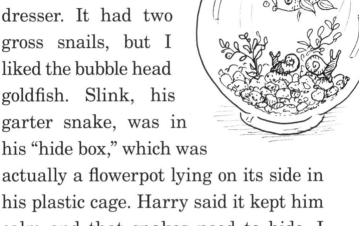 actually a flowerpot lying on its side in his plastic cage. Harry said it kept him calm and that snakes need to hide. I was glad Slink was asleep. I saw just his greenish-yellow-striped tail sticking out. Snakes give me the creeps!

I walked over to Harry's bookcase where there were three old Tootsie Rolls. The wrappers were off. We had used them in our "Deadly Skit" for cigars when the three kings smoked.

"Come over here by the window," Harry said.

"On my way!" I replied, but I walked slowly. I was still looking at Harry's stuff. Quickly I bypassed the wiener fossil and green slime saucer. "That skit we did about not smoking was so cool."

"It was!" Harry agreed. "Especially the part where we keeled over and pretended to be dead!"

"You and Song Lee were dead fish in our Thanksgiving play, too. I remember, I got to be Squanto and save the Pilgrims from starvation."

Harry put two thumbs up.

"Hey, what's this?" I asked, holding up a black spider ring with a big blotch of red.

"Oh, that was a goof. I put too much fingernail polish on it. It was supposed to be a wedding ring for Song Lee. I made her another one."

The thought of a black widow made me cringe, so I stepped away. There was a peanut can I loved to open. As soon as I took off the lid, a green python snake went flying into the air! Harry immediately caught it with one hand.

"Get over here, Dougo!" Harry said. "There's crazy stuff going on in the backyard!"

"Coming! Coming!" But I still dragged my feet because there was so much more to check out in Harry's room.

Harry had his artwork on the wall. My favorite was the one completely

covered with hundreds of green blades of grass. He used only one crayon. There were two holes in it for night crawlers. The art teacher had loved it!

Song Lee's valentine with the red velvet bow was on his bulletin board. And the secret pal note I wrote to him in second grade was pinned next to it.

A huge collection of pencil stub people was in a shoebox. I noticed Harry had

added a few, but Radio
Man, with two gold
button eyes and paper
clip antennas, was
always on top.

"*Dougo!!*"

"Be there in one sec,
Harry!" I said.

And that was when I noticed something *brand new* up on his wall.

Something that was about to ruin
my life!

Socked in the Stomach

"This new?" I said, pointing to the wooden plaque hanging on Harry's wall. It had a gold-plated handsaw on top. His father's name, Fred Spooger, was engraved on it. Just below were the words "Employee of the Year at Belcherville Hardware and Supply."

"Yeah! Dad got it at a banquet last week and gave it to me. He knew I liked the gold handsaw."

"Awesome!" I said, stepping over a long stuffed python and a crocodile to get to Harry.

I sat on my knees and squatted down next to him. Harry slowly lifted up his window with both hands. We poked our heads out just enough so we could spy into that mystery house's backyard and hopefully . . . not be seen. Two ladies were trimming overgrown bushes with clippers. I looked down to the right, along Harry's driveway. His parents were lying on the ground under his grandma's red pickup truck just in front of their garage. All I could see were their legs and feet sticking out. They were both repairing something underneath the truck. Their open toolbox was nearby in the driveway.

"I've got some exciting news!" I finally said.

"What?" Harry's eyes were still glued on the backyard action.

"There's a new house for sale right across the street from me! It's perfect for your family. Do you know yet when you might be able to buy a house?"

And *that's* when Harry dropped the bomb.

"My parents bought a house already."

"What? *Where?*"

Harry mumbled something.

"What did you say?" I asked.

"Belcherville."

"Belcherville?"

"It's where my dad's hardware store is. He's a manager now."

I felt like I just got socked in the stomach.

"Harry! That's in another town! It might as well be another galaxy! We won't be in fourth grade together!"

Harry wasn't paying any attention. "Look, Dougo, that six-footer who was vacuuming . . . is digging up something in the backyard now!"

He was *still* looking out his window.

I tapped him on the shoulder.

Ten times!

"You're moving?" I choked out.

Harry finally turned and looked at me. "Yeah, I am, but not until school is out, sometime next week."

"Next week?" I repeated.

My eyes were bulging out of their sockets!

"We still have a few more days to do fun stuff and be detectives," he added.

I shook my head back and forth . . .

I had no more words.

I just got up and headed for the door.

"Wait, Dougo! We're about to crack the case of the mystery house!"

I felt like cracking him over the head with his long stuffed python! His moving was no biggie to him! Our friendship was over!

Sawed in half!

I made a face when I passed by that wooden plaque.

Belcherville?

As soon as I got outside, I kicked the kickstand as hard as I could and jumped onto my bike. Harry immediately showed up at the door. "*Dougo!* You can't leave now. I know who that was vacuuming. You know her too!"

I didn't even turn around when he

shouted, "It's Mrs. Bernbotham! The substitute teacher! She's planting a tree in that hole!"

I kept pedaling as fast as I could, down the street and back to my house.

Harry's Horrible News!

I didn't feel like going to school on Monday, but Mom made me.

My life was over.

Harry was moving in two more days, and he acted like it didn't even matter!

When I got to school, Harry ambushed me at the playground. He was carrying a rolled-up bag of Epsom salts. I figured it was for our teacher.

"Boy, did you miss out on the biggest

mystery. Guess who moved in next door on Sunday?"

"Mrs. Bernbotham?" I moaned.

"Noooo! The Hammouds! They just came to America from Syria. A group of people from our town are sponsoring them. The older kids know some English already. I played with Mohammed in his backyard all weekend. He showed me where a mole and some gray tree frogs were living. I gave him some milkweed leaves from my yard just in case a caterpillar shows up."

I looked down at the playground as

I listened to Harry go on and on. He didn't mention one single thing about our not being in fourth grade together.

"And they asked me to stay for lunch on Sunday. Mrs. Hammoud brought out a big round beautiful tray of food and set it on the floor! We all sat around it in a cool circle and used small pieces of flat bread to scoop up yogurt and scrambled eggs. It was delicious! There were green olives, tomato slices, and dates, too!"

Harry kept raving about his new neighbors.

"The four older ones will be coming to South School next fall. Mohammed is our age—he'll be in fourth grade next year. Isn't that cool?"

"Cool for who?" I snapped. "You won't even be here."

Just then Song Lee and Ida rushed over.

Sid was right behind them.

The girls were wearing skirts. Ida was busy doing pirouettes and twirling. Song Lee had on that lightbulb necklace and the wedding spider ring that Harry made for her.

He noticed right away.

"You look pretty!" Harry said, flashing a toothy smile.

Song Lee beamed.

"Want to play four square, guys?" Sid said. "I got a new ball from my stepdad."

"No thanks," I replied.

"Is something the matter, Doug?" Song Lee asked. "You look sad."

As soon as she said that, my eyes got watery, so I wiped them quickly with my shirt sleeve. "Harry's moving," I said.

Song Lee covered her mouth. "Ohhhhhh no!"

Ida stopped dancing. "You're moving?"

Sidney dropped his new ball. "Moving where?" he said, not even chasing it when it rolled.

"Belcherville."

"Belcherville? That's another town!" Sidney wrapped his arms around Harry and trapped him. "You can't fly the coop, *Harry the Canary!*" he shouted. "I won't let you go!"

Harry chuckled as he pressed his fist into Sid's head. "*Sid the Squid*! You're okay!"

Sidney suddenly let Harry go. "I won't miss your knuckle noogies," he groaned.

Song Lee's eyes began to fill up with

tears just as Mary joined us. Mary noticed Harry's Epsom salts right away. "You're not giving that to Mrs. Flaubert, are you?"

Harry tapped his bag. "Grandma uses these salts for her tired feet when she soaks in the tub. Our teacher will love them."

Mary made a face. "A half-used bag?"

"Wanted to make sure they were good, Mare. They are!" he replied.

"Harry's moving to Belcherville!" Sid interrupted.

Mary blew up her bangs. "Stop joking, Sidney LaFleur!" she replied. "It's not funny."

ZuZu and Dexter came over and joined us.

"Joking about what?" ZuZu asked.

"Not joking," Sidney said.

Harry made it history. "Sid's right, Mare. I'm moving. Kind of exciting because my parents have been saving for a new house for a long time. You guys will have to come visit me this summer."

"You're *moving*?" Dexter groaned. "Man, we're gonna have no fun without you!"

"You'll bring the music!" Harry said. Then he and Dexter did some dance moves together.

"We're supposed to be together in Mr. Ollie's fourth grade class," Mary objected. "He does all kinds of science. That's your favorite subject, Harry, after recess and gym! Do you have to move? Can't you convince your parents to let you stay with your grandma?"

"Mare . . ." Harry started dancing with her. "My dad is building me a club-house. You guys can come visit!"

When the morning bell rang, Song Lee lined up next to Harry and me. "I will miss you, Harry," she said softly. "Will you write to me?"

Harry made his eyebrows go up and down. "Sure will!" he replied. "I'll write you a poem—a second verse about brown."

Song Lee couldn't help but giggle. She remembered Harry's color poem.

I remembered it too. His original verse said, "Feel the cow doo-doo cool off your piggies."

As we filed into school for the last time that year, our teacher greeted

us with a big smile. But I sure didn't have one. My best friend might as well be moving to the moon. He was never going to be in my class again.

Ever!

And he wasn't even sad about it.

The Last Day of Third Grade

That last half day we didn't have to do any work. Most of the activities were fun except for the square dancing in the gym. I'm not crazy about that, but Harry loved dancing with Song Lee. Mrs. Flaubert put on rock-and-roll records so we could dance to those, too. Dexter played his guitar when it was an Elvis song.

Harry got to go around South School and say goodbye to people like Mr.

Cardini, the principal, Mr. Scooghammer, our computer teacher, and Mr. Beausoleil, our custodian. Harry said he kissed Mrs. Funderburke, our cook, and Mrs. Michaelsen, the librarian, on their hands. Harry said they were like royalty.

We played the old board games that were kept in our classroom closet for forty-seven years. Monopoly with the wooden hotels and houses was the most popular. Clue with the real rope and metal pipe was second. Lots of kids just wanted to draw. Every time I looked over, Harry wasn't sad at all. He was having fun and laughing most of the time.

Hardy har har, I thought.

But I didn't laugh once.

Mary's mom brought in five cheese pizzas and some island punch. Mary said she persuaded her mom to add a sixth gourmet pizza. That one had eggplant on it and looked gross!

Mary and the teacher were the only ones who took a slice of it. (And Mr. Cardini, who stopped in to wish everyone a great summer.)

Mrs. Flaubert loved her gift certificate and our class card. She even loved Harry's Epsom salts, and his note that said she was the best teacher in the universe. It must have had one hundred silver and gold stars on it.

In return, Mrs. Flaubert gave Harry the tarantula poster that our  class won on field day. Mary was psyched to get rid of that hairy picture. Harry said he'd hang it up in his new bedroom. When the teacher handed it to him, he gave her a bear hug.

"I love you, Miss Mackle," he said.

The teacher didn't even correct him. She just said, "I love you too, Harry."

Lots of kids made cards for Harry that day. Song Lee's was the best. It had flowers and hearts on it. She even made little windows on the card that opened up and had pictures of all the creepy crawly things Harry had brought to class, like Charles the spider and Edward the earwig.

I was too bummed to make Harry a card.

He didn't say he was going to miss

me or anything. He just played with different kids all morning.

Instead of celebrating the end of school, we left class that day barely talking. I thought Harry might call me that night, but he didn't. Mom said he was probably busy packing. She said it was a lot of work to move.

On Thursday morning, Harry finally called.

Harry Says Goodbye

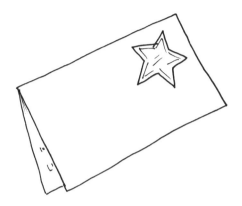

Thursday morning, Mom handed me the phone.

"It's Harry," she whispered.

I grabbed it and said hi right away.

"Hey, Dougo," Harry said. "Can you come over? We're getting ready to go to Belcherville and I wanted to say goodbye."

"Come over now?" I asked.

"Yes!"

Mom nodded.

"Sure!" I said. I missed him already, and it had just been two days.

"Neato," Harry replied. "I'll be waiting."

I raced outside and jumped onto my bike.

As I pedaled by the school, I looked at the empty lot next to it. Harry was the one who first asked the teacher if that could be a nature area. He got all of us involved, and now it *was* one! Anybody could visit the kingdom of mushrooms there, or even see Harry's old hideout. I couldn't imagine life without him.

There were memories of Harry everywhere!

Even yesterday when we were at the grocery store, and Mom was getting herself a cup of coffee. Right when she opened up a small plastic creamer, I thought of Harry. He had given one to Song Lee for the dragon she made. It was an "I'm sorry" gift for saying her papier-mâché dragon was stupid.

As I rounded the corner to Harry's house, I spotted two vehicles parked out in front. When I got closer, I could see his parents were already in the car. It was loaded down with lots of stuff. Grandma Spooger was in her red truck waiting. The back was packed with boxes, a broom, a vacuum cleaner, and Harry's big stuffed animals. The Goog was in a cat carrier next to Harry on the stoop. He was sitting there, waiting for me. There

was something in Harry's hand. I had
something in my pocket.

I skidded to a stop and dropped my
bike.

Harry jumped up and hugged me.

"Dougo!" he exclaimed.

"Harry!" I said, hugging him back.

We didn't let go.

The Goog kept meowing and peeking
out of his carrier.

"I didn't want to say goodbye to you,"
Harry said. "I kept putting it off. It was
easier *not* to talk about it. All I had to
do was think about something else. But
now that it's time for me to go . . . it feels
really . . . *horrible*."

Harry's voice shook a little.

I could tell he *was* going to miss
me.

But I couldn't say anything. I knew if I did, I'd start crying. I wanted to be brave like one of Harry's spiders that lived in caves.

We finally sat down on his grandma's stoop, but just for a moment. He handed me a piece of paper that was folded in half. It had one gold star on it.

Then he put his arm around me.

"Read it later, Dougo," he said. "I'm sorry about the one star. I wanted to use a thousand, but I ran out."

"No problem," I said. "One is cool."

Harry tapped fists with me.

"*Come on, Bud!*" Mr. Spooger called out. "Time to get this show on the road! You and Doug can plan lots of sleepovers this summer."

"*I'm coming!*" Harry hollered back.

Then he gave me one last knuckle noogie, picked up the cat carrier, and headed for the truck.

Just as I got up, I remembered I had something for him, too.

"*Wait, Harry!*" I yelled, and ran after him. Harry immediately stopped and turned around.

The Goog was still meowing. He hated being cooped up!

I reached deep into my pocket and pulled out my Safety Patrol Cadet badge. "We were supposed to be cadets together in fourth grade, remember?" I said. "I want you to have mine. So here's one star for *you!*"

"That's the coolest thing!" Harry said, pinning it on himself right away. "It reminds me of the bronze star my great granddad got in World War II. Thanks, Dougo. You're the best!"

"No," I said. "*You* are!"

Harry wiped his eyes as he took off. He jumped in the cab of his grandma's truck and rolled down the window. "See ya soon!" he yelled.

"See ya . . . soon." I waved as they pulled away from the curb and headed for Belcherville.

I slowly walked back up the stone path to his house and plopped down on his grandma's stoop. Then I unfolded Harry's short note and read it. It was only one sentence.

And that was when I bawled.

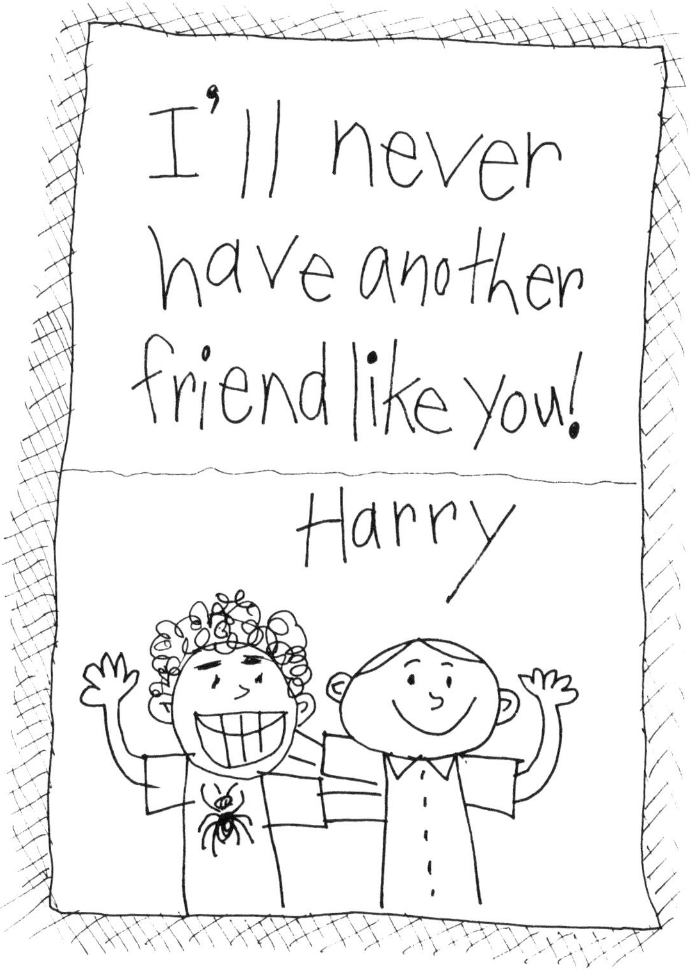
I'll never have another friend like you!
Harry

Harry was gone.

I sat there for ten long minutes on his grandma's stoop, just feeling sad. It was too hard to leave.

When I finally looked up, a tall, dark-haired boy about my age was walking toward me. He was holding a small box.

"Harry here?" he asked with a big smile.

"No. He's . . . gone. Did you move in next door?"

"Yes."

"What's in there?" I said, pointing to his box. There were little holes on top.

The boy sat down next to me and removed the lid.

"A caterpillar!" I said.

"Caterpillar," the boy repeated.

The box had milkweed leaves and

a purple flower inside, with a capful of water. He was taking good care of it.

"My name is Doug," I said. "What's your name?"

"Mohammed," he answered. Then he handed me his box so I could take a closer look.

He trusted me.

Making a new friend felt really good.

"Harry likes creepy crawly things," I said.

Mohammed nodded and smiled.

He did too!

"You're going to be in fourth grade with me," I added. "That's so cool!"

Mohammed put two thumbs up.

And I smiled back. Then I thought to myself, maybe . . . I could write stories about Harry this summer. I could start from the very beginning with second grade. . . .

Harry sits next to me
in Room 2B. He looks
like any other second
grader except for one
thing. Harry likes to
do horrible things.
When I first met Harry
out on the playground,
he had a shoebox. I
asked him, "What's in there?"
"Something. What's your name?"
"Doug", I said.

Acknowledgments

It's hard to believe that Harry has been in second and third grade now for thirty years . . . and that the first Harry book was published in 1988! So it is with much love, and sadness, that I write my last Horrible Harry book—the thirty-seventh one—but, it is time.

I have so many wonderful people to thank for making the Horrible Harry series possible. First of all, its creators—my students!

During the twenty-seven years I taught elementary school, I met so many wonderful characters. The seeds for my Harry stories come from those years being in the classroom. The characters are composites of my most memorable students.

None of these stories would have reached the printed page if it hadn't been for my editors at Viking.

Nancy Paulsen was the person who first envisioned the Horrible Harry series. Chapter one of *Horrible Harry in Room 2B* was actually a picture book manuscript I had written and sent to her.

Nancy said the character was so strong—would I think about putting him in a different format, like an early chapter book for young readers? I loved her idea and jumped in! The stories were launched from that point on, and two early episodic books—*Green Slime* and *Ant Invasion*—followed. So my biggest hug and thank-you goes to Nancy!

And my heartfelt appreciation goes to Regina Hayes, who published my Harry stories for thirty years!

Frank Remkiewicz, my talented first illustrator, made the characters come to life! Because I spend a lot of time writing dialogue in my stories and very little on description, I never said what Harry looked like, just that he had bushy eyebrows. It was a joy to see the first sketches. Frank created Harry with his reddish hair, many-pocketed jacket, jeans, and sneakers. And Harry's expression was "Let's do this!" Song Lee, Doug, Sidney, Ida, and Mary were immediately recognizable to me—what a stroke of magic Frank used in those first twenty-two Harry books! He added so much fun and humor in his illustrations. I can't thank you enough, Frank!

Amy Wummer was the illustrator who continued the special characters Frank created but unleashed them with new energy. She especially brought Mary to life with all her pouty expressions, and Dexter, the passionate Elvis fan! Her details always added to the story. Thank you, Amy, for the last fifteen wonderful books!

Cathy Hennessy edited many of my early Horrible Harry books. Some of my favorites with her were *Moves Up to Third Grade* and *Dragon War*! Thank you so much, Cathy!

Jane Seiter worked with me on a few Harry books—the dungeon story about a new suspension room at South School was one of my favorites. And Liz Breckinridge enthusiastically helped on several others—*Kickball Wedding* and some Song Lee books.

Catherine Frank began editing the Harry books that started with *Locked Closet*. These Harry stories were more complex and with one plot—stories like *The Goog, Takes the Cake, Triple Revenge, Cracks the Code, On the Ropes,* and *The June Box.* Even when she took time off to have her son Spencer, she managed to help me create *Drop of Doom*— another favorite of mine! Thank you, Catherine, for the special dozen we worked on together!

When Catherine left Viking, Leila Sales became my editor, and edited *Scarlet Scissors, Hallway Bully, Stolen Cookie*, and *Battle of the Bugs*. These Harry stories involved sensitive issues like jealousy, bullying, stealing, and having lice. Thank you, Leila, for encouraging these important stories!

Maggie Rosenthal and I worked together on the last two Harry's, which were both filled with strong emotions—*Field Day Revenge* and *Says Goodbye*. Maggie was always so appreciative and supportive! Thank you, dear Maggie!

And a special appreciation for my long-time copyeditor, Janet Pascal, who helped me the most with my Harry editing.

Over the past thirty years I've visited hundreds of schools and got to meet some of my best Horrible Harry readers. Some schools I visit every year.

What a joy it is to meet the new group of second- or third-grade readers who have read so many of my

Horrible Harry stories! Their questions always keep me up on what's important to them.

Two of their questions I'll reanswer here.

What is the theme of the Horrible Harry stories?

Friendship. How good friends help each other through their day, and forgive one another.

And the second question—how come you never take us to Harry's house?

Well, in this last book I do, and we even meet his parents, although just half of them. ☺

Thank you, my dearest readers!

Finally, hugs and thank-yous to my family. For my daughters, Emily and Jennifer, who both managed my author visits and website and have always been so supportive. For my precious grandkids, Jake, Kenna, Gabby, Saylor, and Holden, who grew up reading all the Harry books and whose comments and questions made me a better writer. For my lifelong friends, Terry, Robin, and Charla, who have been with me since our early school years in Albany, California—and who inspired the school friendship of Harry and Doug.

And big hugs to my dearest friends, the Al Kalaf family, who moved to America just three years ago: Maher, Najah, Mohammed, Feryal, Abdul, Rasha, Qablan, Zaher, and Saher, who inspired the ending to this last Harry book.

And lastly, my beloved husband, Rufus, who has been my editor 24/7, and best friend. Thank you for all your help and encouragement with the Horrible Harry stories. I love you!